Welcome to FlowSong

created by A.C. Hart

An Introduction to FlowSong

For my nephew, Aidan. ♡

May you always have the courage to

follow your heart compass home.

◆ FriesenPress

Suite 300 - 990 Fort St
Victoria, BC, V8V 3K2
Canada

www.friesenpress.com

ISBN
978-1-5255-4652-5 (Hardcover)
978-1-5255-4653-2 (Paperback)
978-1-5255-4654-9 (eBook)

1. Juvenile Fiction

Distributed to the trade by The Ingram Book Company

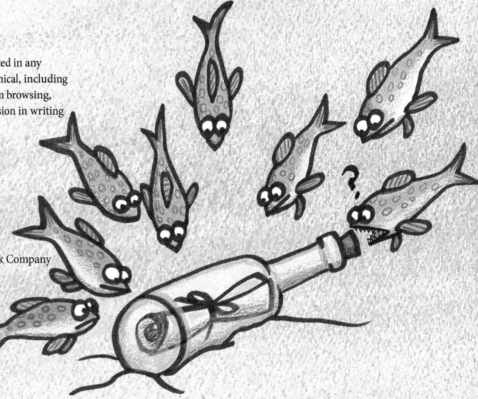

Hey kids! Welcome to FlowSong!

My name is Mojo and I'll be your guide. When you see me with this music note, ask your parents to SING that part of the book with you!

FlowSong books are all supported by online resources. Simply go to FlowSong.com to hear the author read and sing your book to you. Find out more about Flo's exciting adventures in the upcoming 10-book series, FlowSong: an Illustrated Epic in 9½ Parts

Enjoy your FlowSong adventure!

Xing Xing and Dhi lived under the sea
with Sam the Clam. They were happy and free.

Every day Flo and her best friend Mojo
dove into the Sound. Mojo leapt from his bowl

Where he lived on a shelf in Flo's very
pretty red room on Home Street in
Amoga City on the coast near the ocean

of the United States,

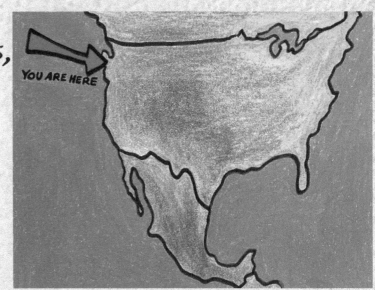

North America,

Earth,

Milky Way,

5

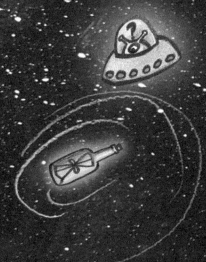

They all LOVE to SING! Guided by Xing Xing
they aim their hearts towards their goal
with all of their might, then sing magic
sounds and dissolve into light.

Riding the Friend-Ship, captained by Flo, the

music transports them where they want to go.

EXPLORING!

DISCOVERING!

LEARNING!

Fish of the
Northern Seas

and GROWING!

bravely **CREATING!** with no way of knowing what lies beyond the next breath or heartbeat but always home in time for bed at Hume Street.

Sam the Clam sang tenor and Xing Xing soprano,
Mojo played bass and Dhi played piano.

12

Flo kept the rhythm and guided the band
for she was wise and had seen, firsthand,
many a moment both heavy and light. She
protected her friends on their magical flight.

13

Together, the GloHearts
SING, brave and bold
using eight sounds to
turn lead into gold.

15

They sing the sound UH that
goes down through their feet

Then OOH in the low belly,
warm and sweet.

They sing *OH* in the stomach
and feel power start

Then sing *AH* in their chests
and open the heart.

Singing A in the throat,
soaring up to the sky,

Then, through the forehead,
they sing the sound I.

Followed by singing
E in the crown,
then the crystalline

HUME that flows down
around their whole bodies,
sung to a tune YOU might know!

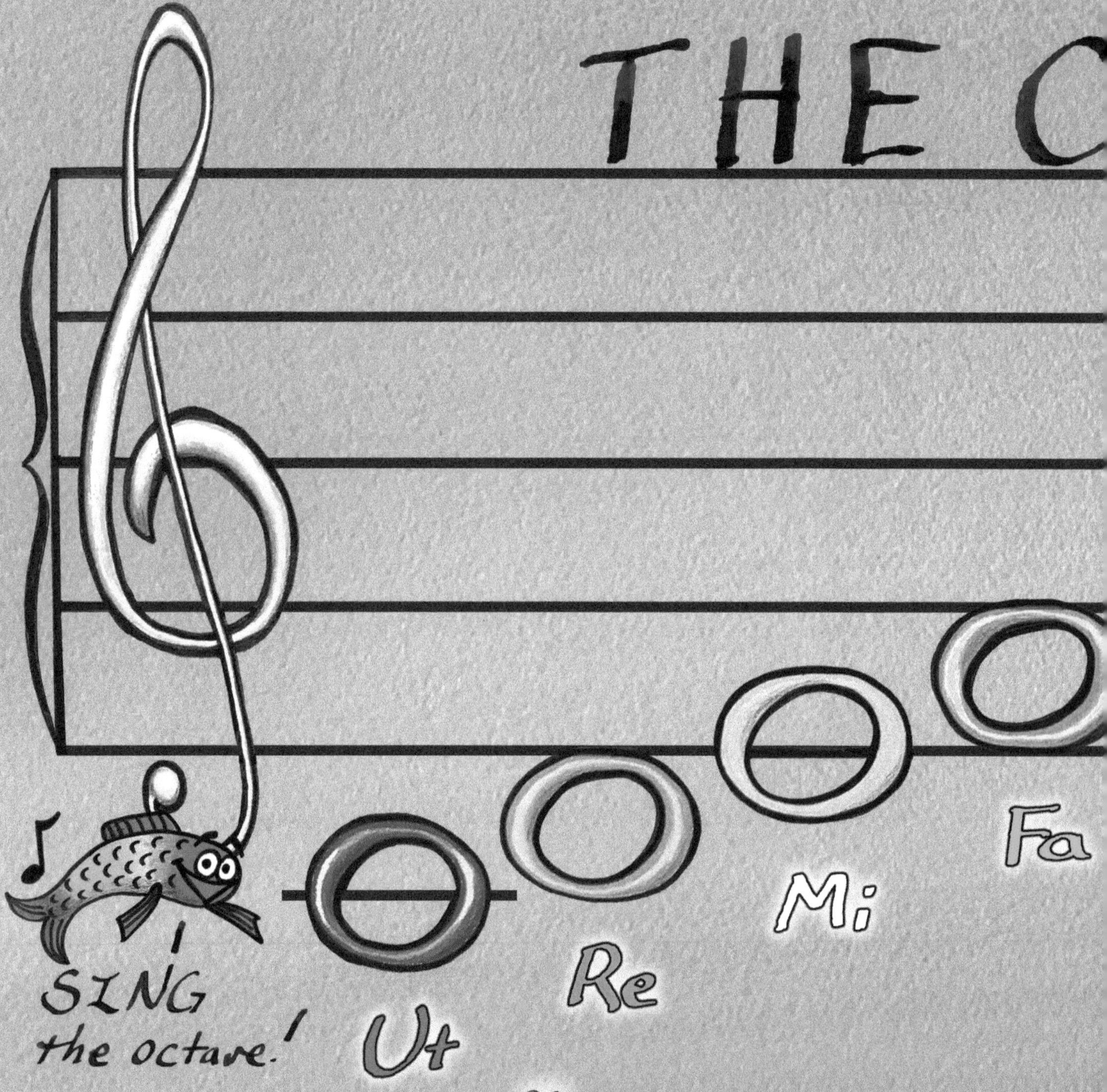
THE C
SING the octave!
Ut
Re
Mi
Fa

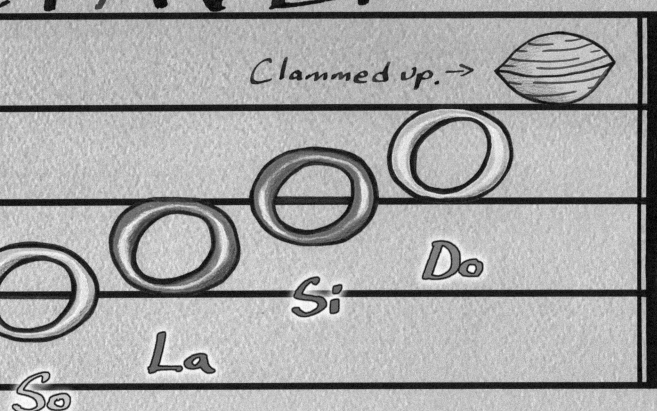

Would YOU like to travel to faraway places?

Perhaps like to paint people's interesting faces?

Or be a chef? Or sing in a band?

Be a dentist, a dog trainer, or a stagehand?

Whatever it is that YOU want to do,
these magical sounds could help you, too.
Create what YOU want! The fun never ends!
Just like with Flo and her four fishy friends.

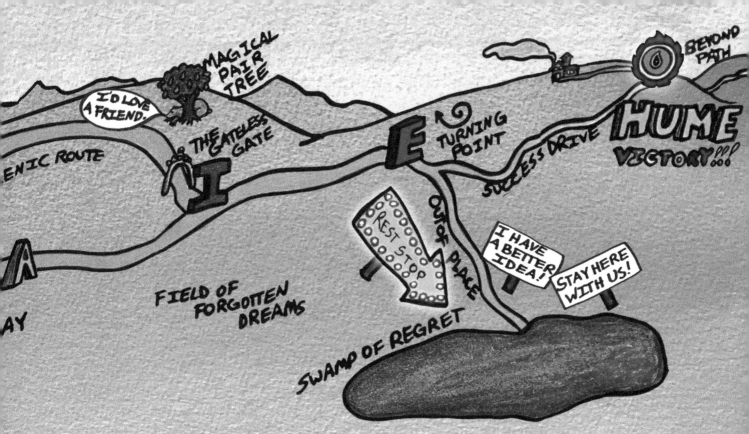

Are you ready now to give it a try?

Do you want to spread your wings and fly?

Use all the powers of your imagination

When focusing on your heart-felt creation.

You can create what YOU want. Your choice!

When you have it, now say in a loud, happy voice,

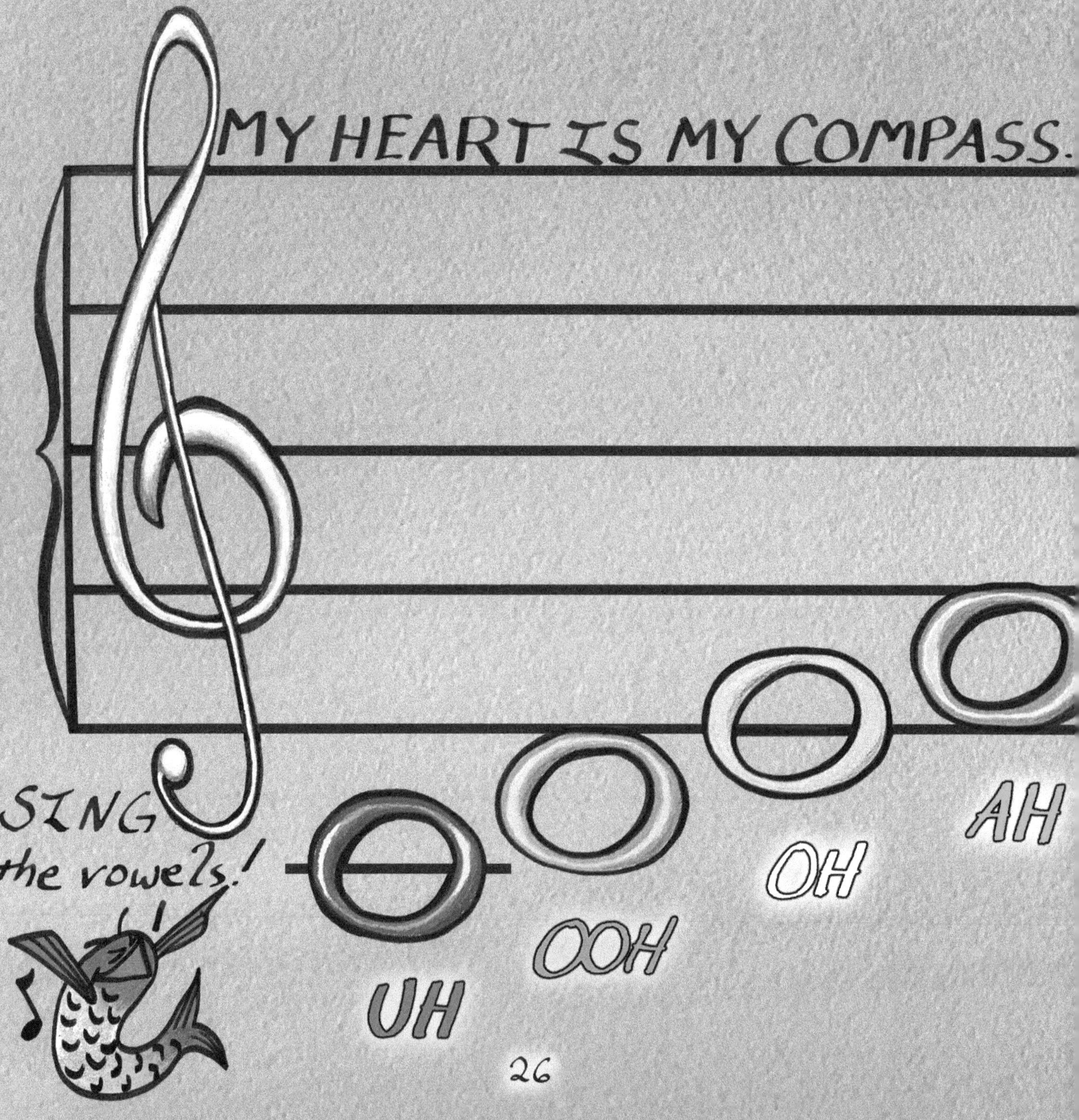
MY HEART IS MY COMPASS.
SING the vowels!
UH
OOH
OH
AH

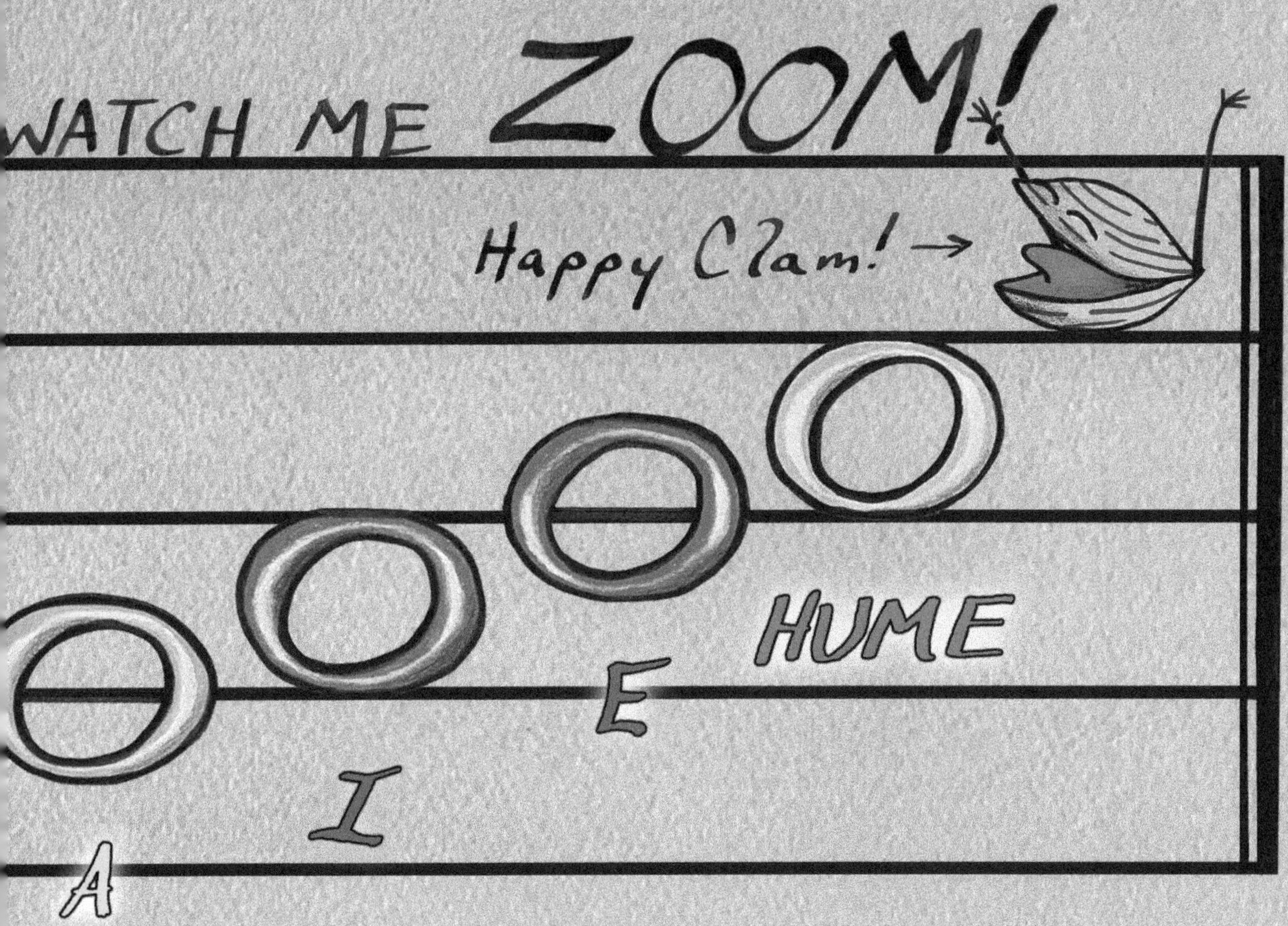
WATCH ME ZOOM!
Happy Clam! →
HUME
E
I
A

It's just the beginning of the magical tales
Of Flo and her buddies, so ready your sails!
When the Friend-Ship hoists anchor there's
no telling where they'll travel to next.
You can go if you dare. Your dreams can
be real. They're not just in your head.
Have fun, and make sure you're
home in time for bed.

29

31

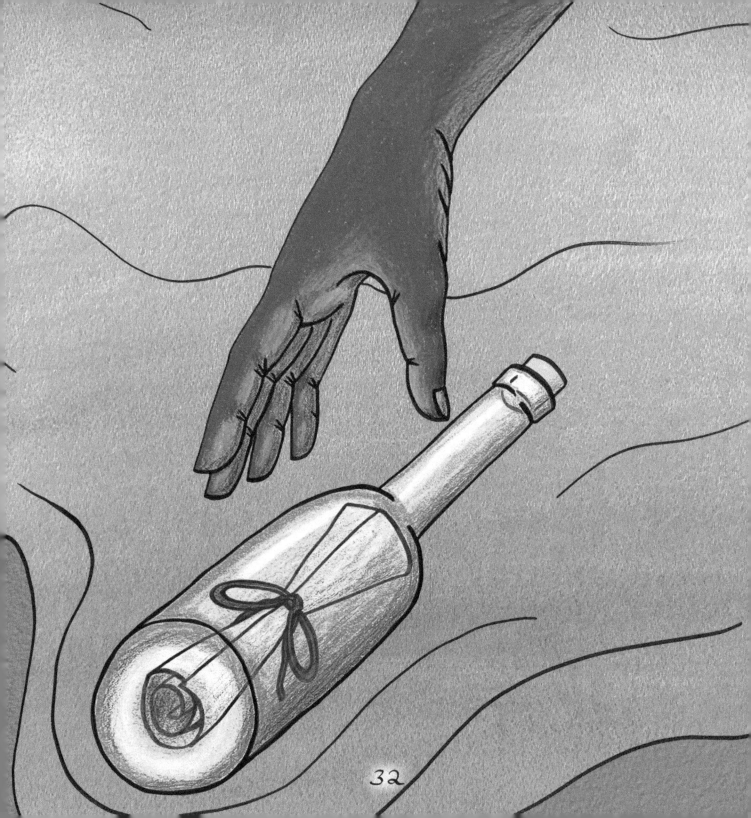

Dear Friend-on-the-Shore
Did you hear what was said? Your dreams can be real. They're not just in your head. The creative flow is where you belong. We'll see you there.
Love, ♡
Flo Song
P.S. Wanna be pen pals? My address is on the back! xoxo

A special thanks to Mom and Dad, Eli Harris, Lar Short, and the GEMs. Without them this book would not have been possible.

FlowSong 972
P.O. Box
El Prado, NM
87529

FlowSong

GET INTO THE FLO

The GloHearts Program

Your purchase directly supports creative education for children. For more information about our charitable giving program, please go to:

FlowSong.com/GloHearts

CPSIA information can be obtained
at www.ICGtesting.com
Printed in the USA
BVHW020226050921
615966BV00002B/5